DEATH COMES FOR THE
ARCHBISHOP

———

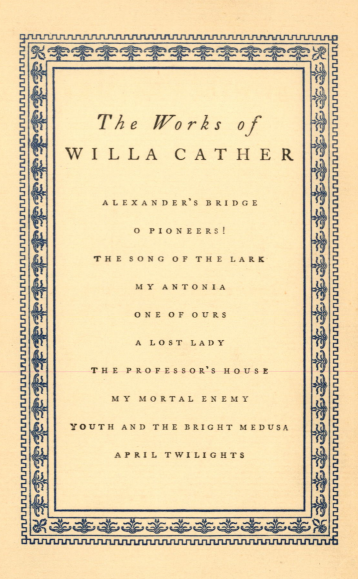

The Works of
WILLA CATHER

ALEXANDER'S BRIDGE

O PIONEERS!

THE SONG OF THE LARK

MY ANTONIA

ONE OF OURS

A LOST LADY

THE PROFESSOR'S HOUSE

MY MORTAL ENEMY

YOUTH AND THE BRIGHT MEDUSA

APRIL TWILIGHTS

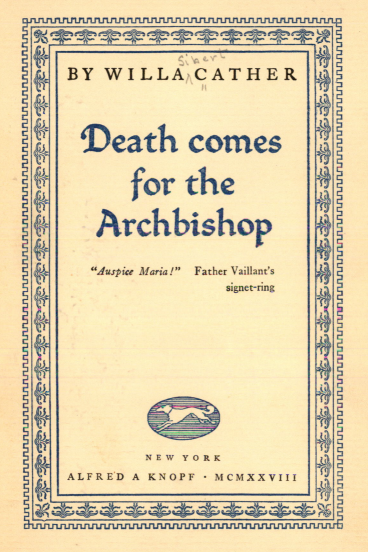

BY WILLA _{Sibert} CATHER

Death comes for the Archbishop

"Auspice Maria!" Father Vaillant's
signet-ring

NEW YORK
ALFRED A KNOPF · MCMXXVIII

CONTENTS

DEATH COMES FOR THE

ARCHBISHOP

———

PROLOGUE

AT ROME

ONE summer evening in the year 1848, three Cardinals and a missionary Bishop from America were dining together in the gardens of a villa in the Sabine hills, overlooking Rome. The villa was famous for the fine view from its terrace. The hidden garden in which the four men sat at table lay some twenty feet below the south end of this terrace, and was a mere shelf of rock, overhanging a steep declivity planted with vineyards. A flight of stone steps connected it with the promenade above. The table stood in a sanded square, among potted orange and oleander trees, shaded by spreading ilex oaks that grew out of the rocks overhead. Beyond the balustrade was the drop into the air, and far below the landscape stretched soft and undulating; there was nothing to arrest the eye until it reached Rome itself.

It was early when the Spanish Cardinal and his guests sat down to dinner. The sun was still good for an hour of supreme splendour, and across the shining folds of country the low profile of the city barely fretted the sky-line — indistinct except for the dome of St. Peter's, bluish grey like the flattened top of a great balloon, just a flash of copper light on its soft metallic surface. The Cardinal had an eccentric preference for beginning his dinner at this time in the late afternoon, when the vehemence of the sun suggested motion. The light was full of action and had a peculiar quality of climax — of splendid finish. It was both intense and soft, with a ruddiness as of much-multiplied candlelight, an aura of red in its flames. It bored into the ilex trees, illuminating their mahogany trunks and blurring their dark foliage; it warmed the bright green of the orange trees and the rose of the oleander blooms to gold; sent congested spiral patterns quivering over the damask and plate and crystal. The churchmen kept their rectangular clerical caps on their heads to protect them from the sun. The three Cardinals wore black cassocks with crimson pipings and crimson buttons, the Bishop a long black coat over his violet vest.

They were talking business; had met, indeed, to discuss an anticipated appeal from the Provincial Council at Baltimore for the founding of an Apostolic Vicarate in New Mexico — a part of North America recently annexed to the United States. This new territory was vague to all of them, even to the missionary Bishop. The Italian and French Cardinals spoke of it as *Le Mexique*, and the Spanish host referred to it as "New Spain." Their interest in the projected Vicarate was tepid, and had to be continually revived by the missionary, Father Ferrand; Irish by birth, French by ancestry — a man of wide wanderings and notable achievement in the New World, an Odysseus of the Church. The language spoken was French — the time had already gone by when Cardinals could conveniently discuss contemporary matters in Latin.

The French and Italian Cardinals were men in vigorous middle life — the Norman full-belted and ruddy, the Venetian spare and sallow and hook-nosed. Their host, Garcia Maria de Allande, was still a young man. He was dark in colouring, but the long Spanish face, that looked out from so many canvases in his ancestral portrait gallery, was in the young Cardinal much modified through his English mother. With his *caffè oscuro* eyes, he had a fresh, pleasant English mouth, and an open manner.

During the latter years of the reign of Gregory XVI, de Allande had been the most influential man at the Vatican; but since the death of Gregory, two years ago, he had retired to his country estate. He believed the reforms of the new Pontiff impractical and dangerous, and had withdrawn from politics, confining his activities to work for the Society for the

3

Propagation of the Faith — that organization which had been so fostered by Gregory. In his leisure the Cardinal played tennis. As a boy, in England, he had been passionately fond of this sport. Lawn tennis had not yet come into fashion; it was a formidable game of indoor tennis the Cardinal played. Amateurs of that violent sport came from Spain and France to try their skill against him.

The missionary, Bishop Ferrand, looked much older than any of them, old and rough — except for his clear, intensely blue eyes. His diocese lay within the icy arms of the Great Lakes, and on his long, lonely horseback rides among his missions the sharp winds had bitten him well. The missionary was here for a purpose, and he pressed his point. He ate more rapidly than the others and had plenty of time to plead his cause, — finished each course with such dispatch that the Frenchman remarked he would have been an ideal dinner companion for Napoleon.

The Bishop laughed and threw out his brown hands in apology. "Likely enough I have forgot my manners. I am preoccupied. Here you can scarcely understand what it means that the United States has annexed that enormous territory which was the cradle of the Faith in the New World. The Vicarate of New Mexico will be in a few years raised to an Episcopal See, with jurisdiction over a country larger than Central and Western Europe, barring Russia. The

Bishop of that See will direct the beginning of momentous things."

"Beginnings," murmured the Venetian, "there have been so many. But nothing ever comes from over there but trouble and appeals for money."

The missionary turned to him patiently. "Your Eminence, I beg you to follow me. This country was evangelized in fifteen hundred, by the Franciscan Fathers. It has been allowed to drift for nearly three hundred years and is not yet dead. It still pitifully calls itself a Catholic country, and tries to keep the forms of religion without instruction. The old mission churches are in ruins. The few priests are without guidance or discipline. They are lax in religious observance, and some of them live in open concubinage. If this Augean stable is not cleansed, now that the territory has been taken over by a progressive government, it will prejudice the interests of the Church in the whole of North America."

"But these missions are still under the jurisdiction of Mexico, are they not?" inquired the Frenchman.

"In the See of the Bishop of Durango?" added Maria de Allande.

The missionary sighed. "Your Eminence, the Bishop of Durango is an old man; and from his seat to Santa Fé is a distance of fifteen hundred English miles. There are no wagon roads, no canals, no navigable rivers. Trade is carried on by means of pack-mules, over treacherous trails. The desert down there has a peculiar horror; I do not mean thirst, nor Indian massacres, which are frequent. The very floor of the world is cracked open into countless canyons and arroyos, fissures in the earth which are sometimes ten feet deep, sometimes a thousand. Up and down these stony chasms the traveller and his mules clamber as best they can. It is impossible to go far in any direction without crossing them. If the Bishop of Durango should summon a disobedient priest by letter, who shall bring the Padre to him? Who can prove that he ever received the summons? The post is carried by hunters, fur trappers, gold seekers, whoever happens to be moving on the trails."

The Norman Cardinal emptied his glass and wiped his lips.

"And the inhabitants, Father Ferrand? If these are the travellers, who stays at home?"

"Some thirty Indian nations, Monsignor, each with its own customs and language, many of them fiercely hostile to each other. And the Mexicans, a naturally devout people. Untaught and unshepherded, they cling to the faith of their fathers."

"I have a letter from the Bishop of Durango, recommending his Vicar for this new post," remarked Maria de Allande.

"Your Eminence, it would be a great misfortune if a native priest were appointed; they have never done well in that field. Besides, this Vicar is old. The new Vicar must be a young man, of strong constitution, full of zeal, and above all, intelligent. He will have to deal with savagery and ignorance, with dissolute priests and political intrigue. He must be a man to whom order is necessary — as dear as life."

The Spaniard's coffee-coloured eyes showed a glint of yellow as he glanced sidewise at his guest. "I suspect, from your exordium, that you have a candidate — and that he is a French priest, perhaps?"

"You guess rightly, Monsignor. I am glad to see that we have the same opinion of French missionaries."

"Yes," said the Cardinal lightly, "they are the best missionaries. Our Spanish fathers made good martyrs, but the French Jesuits accomplish more. They are the great organizers."

"Better than the Germans?" asked the Venetian, who had Austrian sympathies.

"Oh, the Germans classify, but the French arrange! The French missionaries have a sense of proportion and rational adjustment. They are always trying to discover the logical relation of things. It is a passion with them." Here the host turned to the old Bishop again. "But your Grace, why do you neglect this Burgundy? I had this wine brought up from my cellar especially to warm away the chill of your twenty Canadian winters. Surely, you do not gather vintages like this on the shores of the Great Lake Huron?"

The missionary smiled as he took up his untouched glass. "It is superb, your Eminence, but I fear I have lost my palate for vintages. Out there, a little whisky, or Hudson Bay Company rum, does better for us. I must confess I enjoyed the champagne in Paris. We had been forty days at sea, and I am a poor sailor."

"Then we must have some for you." He made a sign to his major-domo. "You like it very cold? And your new Vicar Apostolic, what will he drink in the country of bison and *serpents à sonnettes?* And what will he eat?"

"He will eat dried buffalo meat and frijoles with chili, and he will be glad to drink water when he can get it. He will have no easy life, your Eminence. That country will drink up his youth and strength as it does the rain. He will be called upon for every sacrifice, quite possibly for martyrdom. Only last year the Indian pueblo of San Fernandez de Taos murdered and scalped the American Governor and some dozen other whites. The reason they did not scalp their Padre, was that their Padre was one of the leaders of the rebellion and himself planned the massacre. That is how things stand in New Mexico!"

"Where is your candidate at present, Father?"

PROLOGUE

"He is a parish priest, on the shores of Lake Ontario, in my diocese. I have watched his work for nine years. He is but thirty-five now. He came to us directly from the Seminary."

"And his name is?"

"Jean Marie Latour."

Maria de Allande, leaning back in his chair, put the tips of his long fingers together and regarded them thoughtfully.

"Of course, Father Ferrand, the Propaganda will almost certainly appoint to this Vicarate the man whom the Council at Baltimore recommends."

"Ah yes, your Eminence; but a word from you to the Provincial Council, an inquiry, a suggestion ——"

"Would have some weight, I admit," replied the Cardinal smiling. "And this Latour is intelligent, you say? What a fate you are drawing upon him! But I suppose it is no worse than a life among the Hurons. My knowledge of your country is chiefly drawn from the romances of Fenimore Cooper, which I read in English with great pleasure. But has your priest a versatile intelligence? Any intelligence in matters of art, for example?"

"And what need would he have for that, Monsignor? Besides, he is from Auvergne."

The three Cardinals broke into laughter and refilled their glasses. They were all becoming restive under the monotonous persistence of the missionary.

PROLOGUE

"Listen," said the host, "and I will relate a little story, while the Bishop does me the compliment to drink my champagne. I have a reason for asking this question which you have answered so finally. In my family house in Valencia I have a number of pictures by the great Spanish painters, collected chiefly by my great-grandfather, who was a man of perception in these things and, for his time, rich. His collection of El Greco is, I believe, quite the best in Spain. When my progenitor was an old man, along came one of these missionary priests from New Spain, begging. All missionaries from the Americas were inveterate beggars, then as now, Bishop Ferrand. This Franciscan had considerable success, with his tales of pious Indian converts and struggling missions. He came to visit at my great-grandfather's house and conducted devotions in the absence of the Chaplain. He wheedled a good sum of money out of the old man, as well as vestments and linen and chalices — he would take anything — and he implored my grandfather to give him a painting from his great collection, for the ornamentation of his mission church among the Indians. My grandfather told him to choose from the gallery, believing the priest would covet most what he himself could best afford to spare. But not at all; the hairy Franciscan pounced upon one of the best in the collection; a young St. Francis in meditation, by El Greco, and the model for the saint was one of the very handsome Dukes of Albuquerque. My grandfather protested; tried to persuade the fellow that some picture of the Crucifixion, or a martyrdom, would appeal more strongly to his redskins. What would a St. Francis, of almost feminine beauty, mean to the scalp-takers?

"All in vain. The missionary turned upon his host with a reply which has become a saying in our family: 'You refuse me this picture because it is a good picture. *It is too good for God, but it is not too good for you.*'

"He carried off the painting. In my grandfather's manuscript catalogue, under the number and title of the St. Francis, is written: *Given to Fray Teodocio, for the glory of God, to enrich his mission church at Pueblo de Cia, among the savages of New Spain.*

"It is because of this lost treasure, Father Ferrand, that I happen to have had some personal correspondence with the Bishop of Durango. I once wrote the facts to him fully. He replied to me that the mission at Cia was long ago destroyed and its furnishings scattered. Of course the painting may have been ruined in a pillage or massacre. On the other hand, it may still be hidden away in some crumbling sacristy or smoky wigwam. If your French priest had a discerning eye, now, and were sent to this Vicarate, he might keep my El Greco in mind."

The Bishop shook his head. "No, I can't promise

you — I do not know. I have noticed that he is a man of severe and refined tastes, but he is very reserved. Down there the Indians do not dwell in wigwams, your Eminence," he added gently.

"No matter, Father. I see your redskins through Fenimore Cooper, and I like them so. Now let us go to the terrace for our coffee and watch the evening come on."

The Cardinal led his guests up the narrow stairway. The long gravelled terrace and its balustrade were blue as a lake in the dusky air. Both sun and shadows were gone. The folds of russet country were now violet. Waves of rose and gold throbbed up the sky from behind the dome of the Basilica.

As the churchmen walked up and down the promenade, watching the stars come out, their talk touched upon many matters, but they avoided politics, as men are apt to do in dangerous times. Not a word was spoken of the Lombard war, in which the Pope's position was so anomalous. They talked instead of a new opera by young Verdi, which was being sung in Venice; of the case of a Spanish dancing-girl who had lately become a religious and was said to be working miracles in Andalusia. In this conversation the missionary took no part, nor could he even follow it with much interest. He asked himself whether he had been on the frontier so long that he had quite lost his taste for the talk of clever men.

PROLOGUE

But before they separated for the night Maria de Allande spoke a word in his ear, in English.

"You are *distrait*, Father Ferrand. Are you wishing to unmake your new Bishop already? It is too late. Jean Marie Latour — am I right?"

BOOK ONE

THE VICAR APOSTOLIC

1

THE CRUCIFORM TREE

ONE afternoon in the autumn of 1851 a solitary horseman, followed by a pack-mule, was pushing through an arid stretch of country somewhere in central New Mexico. He had lost his way, and was trying to get back to the trail, with only his compass and his sense of direction for guides. The difficulty was that the country in which he found himself was so featureless — or rather, that it was crowded with features, all exactly alike. As far as he could see, on every side, the landscape was heaped up into monotonous red sand-hills, not much larger than haycocks, and very much the shape of haycocks. One could not have believed that in the number of square miles a man is able to sweep with the eye there could be so many uniform red hills. He had been riding among them since early morning, and the look of the country had no more changed than if he had stood still. He must have travelled through thirty miles of these conical red hills, winding his way in the narrow cracks between them, and he had begun to think that he would never see anything else. They were so exactly like one another that he seemed to be wandering in some geometrical nightmare; flattened cones, they were, more the shape of Mexican ovens than haycocks — yes, exactly the shape of Mexican ovens, red as brick-dust, and naked of vegetation except for small juniper trees. And the junipers, too, were the shape of Mexican ovens. Every conical hill was spotted with smaller cones of juniper, a uniform yellowish green, as the hills were a uniform red. The hills thrust out of the ground so thickly that they seemed to be pushing each other, elbowing each other aside, tipping each other over.

The blunted pyramid, repeated so many hundred times upon his retina and crowding down upon him in the heat, had confused the traveller, who was sensitive to the shape of things.

"*Mais, c'est fantastique!*" he muttered, closing his eyes to rest them from the intrusive omnipresence of the triangle.

When he opened his eyes again, his glance immediately fell upon one juniper which differed in shape from the others. It was not a thick-growing cone, but a naked, twisted trunk, perhaps ten feet high, and at the top it parted into two lateral, flat-lying branches, with a little crest of green in the centre, just above the cleavage. Living vegetation could not present more faithfully the form of the Cross.

The traveller dismounted, drew from his pocket a much worn book, and baring his head, knelt at the foot of the cruciform tree.

Under his buckskin riding-coat he wore a black vest and the cravat and collar of a churchman. A young priest, at his devotions; and a priest in a thousand, one knew at a glance. His bowed head was not that of an ordinary man, — it was built for the seat of a fine intelligence. His brow was open, generous, reflective, his features handsome and somewhat severe. There was a singular elegance about the hands below the fringed cuffs of the buckskin jacket. Everything showed him to be a man of gentle birth — brave, sensitive, courteous. His manners, even when he was alone in the desert, were distinguished. He had a kind of courtesy toward himself, toward his beasts, toward the juniper tree before which he knelt, and the God whom he was addressing.

His devotions lasted perhaps half an hour, and when he rose he looked refreshed. He began talking to his mare in halting Spanish, asking whether she agreed with him that it would be better to push on, weary as she was, in hope of finding the trail. He had no water left in his canteen, and the horses had had none since yesterday morning. They had made a dry camp in these hills last night. The animals were almost at the end of their endurance, but they would not recuperate until they got water, and it seemed best to spend their last strength in searching for it.

On a long caravan trip across Texas this man had had some experience of thirst, as the party with which he travelled was several times put on a meagre water ration for days together. But he had not suffered then as he did now. Since morning he had had a feeling of illness; the taste of fever in his mouth, and alarming seizures of vertigo. As these conical hills pressed closer and closer upon him, he began to wonder whether his long wayfaring from the mountains of Auvergne were possibly to end here. He reminded himself of that cry, wrung from his Saviour on the Cross, "*J'ai soif!*" Of all our Lord's physical sufferings, only one, "I thirst," rose to His lips. Empowered by long training, the young priest blotted himself out of his own consciousness and meditated upon the anguish of his Lord. The Passion of Jesus became for him the only reality; the need of his own body was but a part of that conception.

His mare stumbled, breaking his mood of contemplation. He was sorrier for his beasts than for himself. He, supposed to be the intelligence of the party, had got the poor animals into this interminable desert of ovens. He was afraid he had been absent-minded, had been pondering his problem instead of heeding the way. His problem was how to recover a Bishopric. He was a Vicar Apostolic, lacking a Vicarate. He was thrust out; his flock would have none of him.

The traveller was Jean Marie Latour, consecrated Vicar Apostolic of New Mexico and Bishop of Agathonica *in partibus* at Cincinnati a year ago — and ever since then he had been trying to reach his Vicarate. No one in Cincinnati could tell him how to get to New Mexico — no one had ever been there. Since young Father Latour's arrival in America, a railroad had been built through from New York to Cincinnati; but there it ended. New Mexico lay in the middle of a dark continent. The Ohio merchants knew of two routes only. One was the Santa Fé trail from St. Louis, but at that time it was very dangerous because of Comanche Indian raids. His friends advised Father Latour to go down the river to New Orleans, thence by boat to Galveston, across Texas to San Antonio, and to wind up into New Mexico along the Rio Grande valley. This he had done, but with what misadventures!

His steamer was wrecked and sunk in the Galveston harbour, and he had lost all his worldly possessions except his books, which he saved at the risk of his life. He crossed Texas with a traders' caravan, and approaching San Antonio he was hurt in jumping from an overturning wagon, and had to lie

for three months in the crowded house of a poor
Irish family, waiting for his injured leg to get strong.

It was nearly a year after he had embarked upon
the Mississippi that the young Bishop, at about the
sunset hour of a summer afternoon, at last beheld
the old settlement toward which he had been journey-
ing so long: The wagon train had been going all day
through a greasewood plain, when late in the afternoon the teamsters began shouting that over yonder
was the Villa. Across the level, Father Latour could
distinguish low brown shapes, like earthworks, lying
at the base of wrinkled green mountains with bare
tops, — wave-like mountains, resembling billows
beaten up from a flat sea by a heavy gale; and their
green was of two colors — aspen and evergreen, not
intermingled but lying in solid areas of light and
dark.

As the wagons went forward and the sun sank
lower, a sweep of red carnelian-coloured hills lying
at the foot of the mountains came into view; they
curved like two arms about a depression in the plain;
and in that depression was Santa Fé, at last! A thin,
wavering adobe town . . . a green plaza . . . at one end
a church with two earthen towers that rose high
above the flatness. The long main street began at the
church, the town seemed to flow from it like a stream
from a spring. The church towers, and all the low
adobe houses, were rose colour in that light, — a

little darker in tone than the amphitheatre of red hills behind; and periodically the plumes of poplars flashed like gracious accent marks, — inclining and recovering themselves in the wind.

The young Bishop was not alone in the exaltation of that hour; beside him rode Father Joseph Vaillant, his boyhood friend, who had made this long pilgrimage with him and shared his dangers. The two rode into Santa Fé together, claiming it for the glory of God.

How, then, had Father Latour come to be here in the sand-hills, many miles from his seat, unattended, far out of his way and with no knowledge of how to get back to it?

On his arrival at Santa Fé, this was what had happened: The Mexican priests there had refused to recognize his authority. They disclaimed any knowledge of a Vicarate Apostolic, or a Bishop of Agathonica. They said they were under the jurisdiction of the Bishop of Durango, and had received no instructions to the contrary. If Father Latour was to be their Bishop, where were his credentials? A parchment and letters, he knew, had been sent to the Bishop of Durango, but these had evidently got no farther. There was no postal service in this part of the world; the quickest and surest way to communicate with the Bishop of Durango was to go to him.

THE VICAR APOSTOLIC

So, having travelled for nearly a year to reach Santa Fé, Father Latour left it after a few weeks, and set off alone on horse-back to ride down into Old Mexico and back, a journey of full three thousand miles.

He had been warned that there were many trails leading off the Rio Grande road, and that a stranger might easily mistake his way. For the first few days he had been cautious and watchful. Then he must have grown careless and turned into some purely local trail. When he realized that he was astray, his canteen was already empty and his horses seemed too exhausted to retrace their steps. He had persevered in this sandy track, which grew ever fainter, reasoning that it must lead somewhere.

All at once Father Latour thought he felt a change in the body of his mare. She lifted her head for the first time in a long while, and seemed to redistribute her weight upon her legs. The pack-mule behaved in a similar manner, and both quickened their pace. Was it possible they scented water?

Nearly an hour went by, and then, winding between two hills that were like all the hundreds they had passed, the two beasts whinnied simultaneously. Below them, in the midst of that wavy ocean of sand, was a green thread of verdure and a running stream. This ribbon in the desert seemed no wider than a man could throw a stone,—and it was greener than anything Latour had ever seen, even in his own greenest corner of the Old World. But for the quivering of the hide on his mare's neck and shoulders, he might have thought this a vision, a delusion of thirst.

Running water, clover fields, cottonwoods, acacias, little adobe houses with brilliant gardens, a boy driving a flock of white goats toward the stream, — that was what the young Bishop saw.

A few moments later, when he was struggling with his horses, trying to keep them from overdrinking, a young girl with a black shawl over her head came running toward him. He thought he had never seen a kindlier face. Her greeting was that of a Christian.

"*Ave Maria Purissima, Señor*. Whence do you come?"

"Blessed child," he replied in Spanish, "I am a priest who has lost his way. I am famished for water."

"A priest?" she cried, "that is not possible! Yet I look at you, and it is true. Such a thing has never happened to us before; it must be in answer to my father's prayers. Run, Pedro, and tell father and Salvatore."

———

nature, to arrange and re-create. They spent their ingenuity in the other direction; in accommodating themselves to the scene in which they found themselves. This was not so much from indolence, the Bishop thought, as from an inherited caution and respect. It was as if the great country were asleep, and they wished to carry on their lives without awakening it; or as if the spirits of earth and air and water were things not to antagonize and arouse. When they hunted, it was with the same discretion; an Indian hunt was never a slaughter. They ravaged neither the rivers nor the forest, and if they irrigated, they took as little water as would serve their needs. The land and all that it bore they treated with consideration; not attempting to improve it, they never desecrated it.

As Father Latour and Eusabio approached Albuquerque, they occasionally fell in with company; Indians going to and fro on the long winding trails across the plain, or up into the Sandia mountains. They had all of them the same quiet way of moving, whether their pace was swift or slow, and the same unobtrusive demeanour: an Indian wrapped in his bright blanket, seated upon his mule or walking beside it, moving through the pale new-budding sage-brush, winding among the sand waves, as if it were his business to pass unseen and unheard through a country awakening with spring.

DEATH COMES FOR THE ARCHBISHOP

North of Laguna two Zuñi runners sped by them, going somewhere east on "Indian business." They saluted Eusabio by gestures with the open palm, but did not stop. They coursed over the sand with the fleetness of young antelope, their bodies disappearing and reappearing among the sand dunes, like the shadows that eagles cast in their strong, unhurried flight.

BOOK EIGHT

GOLD UNDER PIKE'S PEAK

I

CATHEDRAL

FATHER VAILLANT had been in Santa Fé nearly three weeks, and as yet nothing had been revealed to him that warranted his Bishop in calling him back from Tucson. One morning Fructosa came into the garden to tell him that lunch would be earlier than usual, as the Bishop was going to ride somewhere that afternoon. Half an hour later he joined his superior in the dining-room.

The Bishop seldom lunched alone. That was the hour when he could most conveniently entertain a priest from one of the distant parishes, an army officer, an American trader, a visitor from Old Mexico or California. He had no parlour — his dining-room served that purpose. It was long and cool, with windows only at the west end, opening into the garden. The green jalousies let in a tempered light. Sunbeams played on the white, rounded walls

239

and twinkled on the glass and silver of the sideboard. When Madame Olivares left Santa Fé to return to New Orleans and sold her effects at auction, Father Latour bought her sideboard, and the diningtable around which friends had so often gathered. Doña Isabella gave him her silver coffee service and candelabra for remembrance. They were the only ornaments of the severe and shadowy room.

The Bishop was already at his place when Father Joseph entered. "Fructosa has told you why we are lunching early? We will take a ride this afternoon. I have something to show you."

"Very good. Perhaps you have noticed that I am a little restless. I don't know when I have been two weeks out of the saddle before. When I go to visit Contento in his stall, he looks at me reprovingly. He will grow too fat."

The Bishop smiled, with a shade of sarcasm on his upper lip. He knew his Joseph. "Ah, well," he said carelessly, "a little rest will not hurt him, after coming six hundred miles from Tucson. You can take him out this afternoon, and I will ride Angelica."

The two priests left Santa Fé a little after midday, riding west. The Bishop did not disclose his objective, and the Vicar asked no questions. Soon they left the wagon road and took a trail running straight south, through an empty greasewood country sloping gradually in the direction of the naked, blue Sandia mountains.

At about four o'clock they came out upon a ridge high over the Rio Grande valley. The trail dropped down a long decline at this point and wound about the foot of the Sandias into Albuquerque, some sixty miles away. This ridge was covered with cone-shaped, rocky hills, thinly clad with piñons, and the rock was a curious shade of green, something between sea-green and olive. The thin, pebbly earth, which was merely the rock pulverized by weather, had the same green tint. Father Latour rode to an isolated hill that beetled over the western edge of the ridge, just where the trail descended. This hill stood up high and quite alone, boldly facing the declining sun and the blue Sandias. As they drew close to it, Father Vaillant noticed that on the western face the earth had been scooped away, exposing a rugged wall of rock — not green like the surrounding hills, but yellow, a strong golden ochre, very much like the gold of the sunlight that was now beating upon it. Picks and crowbars lay about, and fragments of stone, freshly broken off.

"It is curious, is it not, to find one yellow hill among all these green ones?" remarked the Bishop, stooping to pick up a piece of the stone. "I have ridden over these hills in every direction, but this is the only one of its kind." He stood regarding the chip of yellow rock that lay in his palm. As he had a very special way of handling objects that were sacred, he extended that manner to things which he considered beautiful. After a moment of silence he looked up at the rugged wall, gleaming gold above them. "That hill, *Blanchet*, is my Cathedral."

Father Joseph looked at his Bishop, then at the cliff, blinking. "*Vraiment?* Is the stone hard enough? A good colour, certainly; something like the colonnade of St. Peter's."

The Bishop smoothed the piece of rock with his thumb. "It is more like something nearer home — I mean, nearer Clermont. When I look up at this rock I can almost feel the Rhone behind me."

"Ah, you mean the old Palace of the Popes, at Avignon! Yes, you are right, it is very like. At this hour, it is like this."

The Bishop sat down on a boulder, still looking up at the cliff. "It is the stone I have always wanted, and I found it quite by chance. I was coming back from Isleta. I had been to see old Padre Jesus when he was dying. I had never come by this trail, but when I reached Santo Domingo I found the road so washed by a heavy rain that I turned out and decided to try this way home. I rode up here from the west in the late afternoon; this hill confronted me as it confronts us now, and I knew instantly that it was my Cathedral."

"Oh, such things are never accidents, Jean. But it will be a long while before you can think of building."

"Not so very long, I hope. I should like to complete it before I die — if God so wills. I wish to leave nothing to chance, or to the mercy of American builders. I had rather keep the old adobe church we have now than help to build one of those horrible structures they are putting up in the Ohio cities. I want a plain church, but I want a good one. I shall certainly never lift my hand to build a clumsy affair of red brick, like an English coach-house. Our own Midi Romanesque is the right style for this country."

Father Vaillant sniffed and wiped his glasses. "If you once begin thinking about architects and styles, Jean! And if you don't get American builders, whom will you get, pray?"

"I have an old friend in Toulouse who is a very fine architect. I talked this matter over with him when I was last at home. He cannot come himself; he is afraid of the long sea voyage, and not used to horseback travel. But he has a young son, still at his studies, who is eager to undertake the work. Indeed, his father writes me that it has become the young man's dearest ambition to build the first Romanesque church in the New World. He will have studied the right models; he thinks our old churches of the Midi the most beautiful in France. When we are ready, he will come and bring with him a couple of good French stone-cutters. They will certainly be no more expensive than workmen from St. Louis. Now that I have found exactly the stone I want, my Cathedral seems to me already begun. This hill is only about fifteen miles from Santa Fé; there is an up-grade, but it is gradual. Hauling the stone will be easier than I could have hoped for."

"You plan far ahead," Father Vaillant looked at his friend wonderingly. "Well, that is what a Bishop should be able to do. As for me, I see only what is under my nose. But I had no idea you were going in for fine building, when everything about us is so poor — and we ourselves are so poor."

"But the Cathedral is not for us, Father Joseph. We build for the future — better not lay a stone unless we can do that. It would be a shame to any man coming from a Seminary that is one of the architectural treasures of France, to make another ugly church on this continent where there are so many already."

"You are probably right. I had never thought of it before. It never occurred to me that we could have anything but an Ohio church here. Your ancestors helped to build Clermont Cathedral, I remember; two building Bishops de la Tour back in the thirteenth century. Time brings things to pass, certainly. I had no idea you were taking all this so much to heart."

Father Latour laughed. "Is a cathedral a thing to be taken lightly, after all?"

"Oh, no, certainly not!" Father Vaillant moved his shoulders uneasily. He did not himself know why he hung back in this.

The base of the hill before which they stood was already in shadow, subdued to the tone of rich yellow clay, but the top was still melted gold — a colour that throbbed in the last rays of the sun. The Bishop turned away at last with a sigh of deep content. "Yes," he said slowly, "that rock will do very well. And now we must be starting home. Every time I come here, I like this stone better. I could hardly have hoped that God would gratify my personal taste, my vanity, if you will, in this way. I tell you, *Blanchet*, I would rather have found that hill of yellow rock than have come into a fortune to spend in charity. The Cathedral is near my heart, for many reasons. I hope you do not think me very worldly."

As they rode home through the sage-brush silvered by moonlight, Father Vaillant was still wondering why he had been called home from saving souls in Arizona, and wondering why a poor missionary Bishop should care so much about a building. He himself was eager to have the Cathedral begun; but whether it was Midi Romanesque or Ohio German in style, seemed to him of little consequence.

2

A LETTER FROM LEAVENWORTH

THE day after the Bishop and his Vicar rode to the yellow rock the weekly post arrived at Santa Fé. It brought the Bishop many letters, and he was shut in his study all morning. At lunch he told Father Vaillant that he would require his company that evening to consider with him a letter of great importance from the Bishop of Leavenworth.

This letter of many pages was concerned with events that were happening in Colorado, in a part of the Rocky Mountains very little known. Though it was only a few hundred miles north of Santa Fé, communication with that region was so infrequent that news travelled to Santa Fé from Europe more quickly than from Pike's Peak. Under the shadow of that peak rich gold deposits had been discovered within the last year, but Father Vaillant had first heard of this through a letter from France. Word of it had reached the Atlantic coast, crossed to Europe, and come from there back to the Southwest, more quickly than it could filter down through the few hundred miles of unexplored mountains and gorges between Cherry Creek and Santa Fé. While Father Vaillant was at Tucson he had received a letter from his brother Marius, in Auvergne, and was vexed that so much of it was taken up with inquiries about the gold rush to Colorado, of which he had never heard, while Marius gave him but little news of the war in Italy, which seemed relatively near and much more important.

That congested heaping up of the Rocky Mountain chain about Pike's Peak was a blank space on the continent at this time. Even the fur trappers, coming down from Wyoming to Taos with their pelts, avoided that humped granite backbone. Only a few years before, Frémont had tried to penetrate the Colorado Rockies, and his party had come half-starved into Taos at last, having eaten most of their horses. But within twelve months everything had changed. Wandering prospectors had found large deposits of gold along Cherry Creek, and the mountains that were solitary a year ago were now full of people. Wagon trains were streaming westward across the prairies from the Missouri River.

The Bishop of Leavenworth wrote Father Latour that he himself had just returned from a visit to Colorado. He had found the slopes under Pike's Peak dotted with camps, the gorges black with placer miners; thousands of people were living in tents and shacks, Denver City was full of saloons and gambling-rooms; and among all the wanderers and wastrels were many honest men, hundreds of good

Catholics, and not one priest. The young men were adrift in a lawless society without spiritual guidance. The old men died from exposure and mountain pneumonia, with no one to give them the last rites of the Church.

This new and populous community must, for the present, the Kansas Bishop wrote, be accounted under Father Latour's jurisdiction. His great diocese, already enlarged by thousands of square miles to the south and west, must now, on the north, take in the still undefined but suddenly important region of the Colorado Rockies. The Bishop of Leavenworth begged him to send a priest there as soon as possible,— an able one, by all means, not only devoted, but resourceful and intelligent, one who would be at his ease with all sorts of men. He must take his bedding and camp outfit, medicines and provisions, and clothing for the severe winter. At Camp Denver there was nothing to be bought but tobacco and whisky. There were no women there, and no cook stoves. The miners lived on half-baked dough and alcohol. They did not even keep the mountain water pure, and so died of fever. All the living conditions were abominable.

In the evening, after dinner, Father Latour read this letter aloud to Father Vaillant in his study. When he had finished, he put down the closely written pages.

GOLD UNDER PIKE'S PEAK

"You have been complaining of inactivity, Father Joseph; here is your opportunity."

Father Joseph, who had been growing more and more restless during the reading of the letter, said merely: "So now I must begin speaking English again! I can start to-morrow if you wish it."

The Bishop shook his head. "Not so fast. There will be no hospitable Mexicans to receive you at the end of this journey. You must take your living with you. We will have a wagon built for you, and choose your outfit carefully. Tranquilino's brother, Sabino, will be your driver. This, I fear, will be the hardest mission you have ever undertaken."

The two priests talked until a late hour. There was Arizona to be considered; somebody must be found to continue Father Vaillant's work there. Of all the countries he knew, that desert and its yellow people were the dearest to him. But it was the discipline of his life to break ties; to say farewell and move on into the unknown.

Before he went to bed that night Father Joseph greased his boots and trimmed the calloused spots on his feet with an old razor. At the Mexican village of Chimayo, over toward the Truchas mountains, the good people were especially devoted to a little equestrian image of Santiago in their church, and they made him a new pair of boots every few months, insisting that he went abroad at night and wore out his shoes, even on horseback. When Father Joseph stayed there, he used to tell them he wished that, in addition to the consecration of the hands, God had provided some special blessing for the missionary's feet.

He recalled affectionately an incident which concerned this Santiago of Chimayo. Some years ago Father Joseph was asked to go to the *calabozo* at Santa Fé to see a murderer from Chimayo. The prisoner proved to be a boy of twenty, very gentle in face and manner. His name was Ramon Armajillo. He had been passionately fond of cock-fighting, and it was his undoing. He had bred a rooster that never lost a battle, but had slit the necks of cocks in all the little towns about. At last Ramon brought the bird to Santa Fé to match him with a famous cock there, and half a dozen Chimayo boys came along and put up everything they had on Ramon's rooster. The betting was heavy on both sides, and the gate receipts also were to go to the winner. After a somewhat doubtful beginning, Ramon's cock neatly ripped the jugular vein of his opponent; but the owner of the defeated bird, before anyone could stop him, reached into the ring and wrung the victor's neck. Before he had dropped the limp bunch of feathers from his hand, Ramon's knife was in his heart. It all happened in a flash — some of the witnesses even insisted that the death of the man and the death of the cock were simultaneous. All agreed that there was not time for a man to catch his breath between the whirl of the wrist and the gleam of the knife. Unfortunately the American judge was a very stupid man, who disliked Mexicans and hoped to wipe out cock-fighting. He accepted as evidence statements made by the murdered man's friends to the effect that Ramon had repeatedly threatened his life.

When Father Vaillant went to see the boy in his cell a few days before his execution, he found him making a pair of tiny buckskin boots, as if for a doll, and Ramon told him they were for the little Santiago in the church at home. His family would come up to Santa Fé for the hanging, and they would take the boots back to Chimayo, and perhaps the little saint would say a good word for him.

Rubbing oil into his boots by candlelight, Father Vaillant sighed. The criminals with whom he would have to do in Colorado would hardly be of that type, he told himself.

DEATH COMES FOR THE ARCHBISHOP

AUSPICE MARIA!

THE construction of Father Vaillant's wagon took a month. It must be a wagon of very unusual design, capable of carrying a great deal, yet light enough and narrow enough to wind through the mountain gorges beyond Pueblo, — where there were no roads at all except the rocky ravines cut out by streams that flowed full in the spring but would be dry now in the autumn. While his wagon was building, Father Joseph was carefully selecting his stores, and the furnishings for a small chapel which he meant to construct of saplings or canvas immediately upon his arrival at Camp Denver. Moreover, there were his valises full of medals, crosses, rosaries, coloured pictures and religious pamphlets. For himself, he required no books but his breviary and the ordinary of the Mass.

In the Bishop's courtyard he sorted and re-sorted his cargo, always finding a more necessary article for which a less necessary had to be discarded. Fructosa and Magdalena were frequently called upon to help him, and when a box was finally closed, Fructosa had it put away in the woodshed. She had noticed the Bishop's brows contract slightly when he came upon these trunks and chests in his hallway and dining-room. All the bedding and clothing was packed in great sacks of dressed calfskin, which Sabino procured from old Mexican settlers. These were already going out of fashion, but in the early days they were the poor man's trunk.

Bishop Latour also was very busy at this time, training a new priest from Clermont; riding about with him among the distant parishes and trying to give him an understanding of the people. As a Bishop, he could only approve Father Vaillant's eagerness to be gone, and the enthusiasm with which he turned to hardships of a new kind. But as a man, he was a little hurt that his old comrade should leave him without one regret. He seemed to know, as if it had been revealed to him, that this was a final break; that their lives would part here, and that they would never work together again. The bustle of preparation in his own house was painful to him, and he was glad to be abroad among the parishes.

One day when the Bishop had just returned from Albuquerque, Father Vaillant came in to luncheon in high spirits. He had been out for a drive in his new wagon, and declared that it was satisfactory at last. Sabino was ready, and he thought they would start the day after to-morrow. He diagrammed his route on the table-cloth, and went over the catalogue of his equipment. The Bishop was tired and scarcely touched his food, but Father Joseph ate generously, as he was apt to do when fired by a new project.

After Fructosa had brought the coffee, he leaned back in his chair and turned to his friend with a beaming face. "I often think, Jean, how you were an unconscious agent in the hands of Providence when you recalled me from Tucson. I seemed to be doing the most important work of my life there, and you recalled me for no reason at all, apparently. You did not know why, and I did not know why. We were both acting in the dark. But Heaven knew what was happening on Cherry Creek, and moved us like chessmen on the board. When the call came, I was here to answer it — by a miracle, indeed."

Father Latour put down his silver coffee-cup. "Miracles are all very well, Joseph, but I see none here. I sent for you because I felt the need of your companionship. I used my authority as a Bishop to gratify my personal wish. That was selfish, if you will, but surely natural enough. We are countrymen, and are bound by early memories. And that two friends, having come together, should part and go their separate ways — that is natural, too. No, I don't think we need any miracle to explain all this."

Father Vaillant had been wholly absorbed in his preparations for saving souls in the gold camps — blind to everything else. Now it came over him in a flash, how the Bishop had held himself aloof from his activities; it was a very hard thing for Father Latour to let him go; the loneliness of his position had begun to weigh upon him.

Yes, he reflected, as he went quietly to his own room, there was a great difference in their natures. Wherever he went, he soon made friends that took the place of country and family. But Jean, who was at ease in any society and always the flower of courtesy, could not form new ties. It had always been so. He was like that even as a boy; gracious to everyone, but known to a very few. To man's wisdom it would have seemed that a priest with Father Latour's exceptional qualities would have been better placed in some part of the world where scholarship, a handsome person, and delicate perceptions all have their effect; and that a man of much rougher type would have served God well enough as the first Bishop of New Mexico. Doubtless Bishop Latour's successors would be men of a different fibre. But God had his reasons, Father Joseph devoutly believed. Perhaps it pleased Him to grace the beginning of a new era and a vast new diocese by a fine personality. And perhaps, after all, something would remain through the years to come; some ideal, or memory, or legend.

The next afternoon, his wagon loaded and standing ready in the courtyard, Father Vaillant was seated at the Bishop's desk, writing letters to France; a

short one to Marius, a long one to his beloved Philo-
mène, telling her of his plunge into the unknown and
begging her prayers for his success in the world of
gold-crazed men. He wrote rapidly and jerkily,
moving his lips as well as his fingers. When the Bishop
entered the study, he rose and stood holding the
written pages in his hand.

"I did not mean to interrupt you, Joseph, but do
you intend to take Contento with you to Colorado?"

Father Joseph blinked. "Why, certainly. I had
intended to ride him. However, if you have need for
him here ——"

"Oh, no. Not at all. But if you take Contento,
I will ask you to take Angelica as well. They have a
great affection for each other; why separate them
indefinitely? One could not explain to them. They
have worked long together."

Father Vaillant made no reply. He stood looking
intently at the pages of his letter. The Bishop saw a
drop of water splash down upon the violet script
and spread. He turned quickly and went out through
the arched doorway.

At sunrise next morning Father Vaillant set out,
Sabino driving the wagon, his oldest boy riding
Angelica, and Father Joseph himself riding Contento.
They took the old road to the north-east, through the
sharp red sand-hills spotted with juniper, and the

Bishop accompanied them as far as the loop where
the road wound out on the top of one of those conical
hills, giving the departing traveller his last glimpse
of Santa Fé. There Father Joseph drew rein and
looked back at the town lying rosy in the morning
light, the mountain behind it, and the hills close
about it like two encircling arms.

"*Auspice, Maria!*" he murmured as he turned his
back on these familiar things.

The Bishop rode home to his solitude. He was
forty-seven years old, and he had been a missionary
in the New World for twenty years — ten of them
in New Mexico. If he were a parish priest at home,
there would be nephews coming to him for help in
their Latin or a bit of pocket-money; nieces to run
into his garden and bring their sewing and keep an
eye on his housekeeping. All the way home he in-
dulged in such reflections as any bachelor nearing
fifty might have.

But when he entered his study, he seemed to come
back to reality, to the sense of a Presence awaiting
him. The curtain of the arched doorway had scarcely
fallen behind him when that feeling of personal loneliness was gone, and a sense of loss was replaced by
a sense of restoration. He sat down before his desk,
deep in reflection. It was just this solitariness of love
in which a priest's life could be like his Master's.
It was not a solitude of atrophy, of negation, but

of perpetual flowering. A life need not be cold, or devoid of grace in the worldly sense, if it were filled by Her who was all the graces; Virgin-daughter, Virgin-mother, girl of the people and Queen of Heaven: *le rêve suprême de la chair*. The nursery tale could not vie with Her in simplicity, the wisest theologians could not match Her in profundity.

Here in his own church in Santa Fé there was one of these nursery Virgins, a little wooden figure, very old and very dear to the people. De Vargas, when he recaptured the city for Spain two hundred years ago, had vowed a yearly procession in her honour, and it was still one of the most solemn events of the Christian year in Santa Fé. She was a little wooden figure, about three feet high, very stately in bearing, with a beautiful though rather severe Spanish face. She had a rich wardrobe; a chest full of robes and laces, and gold and silver diadems. The women loved to sew for her and the silversmiths to make her chains and brooches. Father Latour had delighted her wardrobe keepers when he told them he did not believe the Queen of England or the Empress of France had so many costumes. She was their doll and their queen, something to fondle and something to adore, as Mary's Son must have been to Her.

These poor Mexicans, he reflected, were not the first to pour out their love in this simple fashion. Raphael and Titian had made costumes for Her in their time, and the great masters had made music for Her, and the great architects had built cathedrals for Her. Long before Her years on earth, in the long twilight between the Fall and the Redemption, the pagan sculptors were always trying to achieve the image of a goddess who should yet be a woman.

Bishop Latour's premonition was right: Father Vaillant never returned to share his work in New Mexico. Come back he did, to visit his old friends, whenever his busy life permitted. But his destiny was fulfilled in the cold, steely Colorado Rockies, which he never loved as he did the blue mountains of the South. He came back to Santa Fé to recuperate from the illnesses and accidents which consistently punctuated his way; came with the Papal Emissary when Bishop Latour was made Archbishop; but his working life was spent among bleak mountains and comfortless mining camps, looking after lost sheep.

Creede, Durango, Silver City, Central City, over the Continental Divide into Utah, — his strange Episcopal carriage was known throughout that rugged granite world.

It was a covered carriage, on springs, and long enough for him to lie down in at night, — Father Joseph was a very short man. At the back was a luggage box, which could be made into an altar when he celebrated Mass in the open, under a pine tree.

He used to say that the mountain torrents were the first road builders, and that wherever they found a way, he could find one. He wore out driver after driver, and his coach was repaired so often and so extensively that long before he abandoned it there was none of the original structure left.

Broken tongues and singletrees, smashed wheels and splintered axles he considered trifling matters. Twice the old carriage itself slipped off the mountain road and rolled down the gorge, with the priest inside. From the first accident of this kind, Father Vaillant escaped with nothing worse than a sprain, and he wrote Bishop Latour that he attributed his preservation to the Archangel Raphael, whose office he had said with unusual fervour that morning. The second time he rolled down a ravine, near Central City, his thigh-bone was broken just below the ·joint. It knitted in time, but he was lamed for life, and could never ride horseback again.

Before this accident befell him, however, he had one long visit among his friends in Santa Fé and Albuquerque, a renewal of old ties that was like an Indian summer in his life. When he left Denver, he told his congregation there that he was going to the Mexicans to beg for money. The church in Denver was under a roof, but the windows had been boarded up for months because nobody would buy glass for them. In his Denver congregation there were men who owned mines and saw-mills and flourishing businesses, but they needed all their money to push these enterprises. Down among the Mexicans, who owned nothing but a mud house and a burro, he could always raise money. If they had anything at all, they gave.

He called this trip frankly a begging expedition, and he went in his carriage to bring back whatever he could gather. When he got as far as Taos, his Irish driver mutinied. Not another mile over these roads, he said. He knew his own territory, but here he refused to risk his neck and the Padre's. There was then no wagon road from Taos to Santa Fé. It was nearly a fortnight before Father Vaillant found a man who would undertake to get him through the mountains. At last an old driver, schooled on the wagon trains, volunteered; and with the help of ax and pick and shovel, he brought the Episcopal carriage safely to Santa Fé and into the Bishop's courtyard.

Once again among his own people, as he still called them, Father Joseph opened his campaign, and the poor Mexicans began taking dollars out of their shirts and boots (favourite places for carrying money) to pay for windows in the Denver church. His petitions did not stop with windows — indeed, they only began there. He told the sympathetic women of Santa Fé and Albuquerque about all the stupid, unnecessary discomforts of his life in Denver, discomforts that amounted to improprieties. It was a part of the Wild West attitude to despise the decencies of life. He told them how glad he was to sleep in good Mexican beds once more. In Denver he lay on a mattress stuffed with straw; a French priest who was visiting him had pulled out a long stem of hay that stuck through the thin ticking, and called it an American feather. His dining-table was made of planks covered with oilcloth. He had no linen at all, neither sheets nor serviettes, and he used his worn-out shirts for face towels. The Mexican women could scarcely bear to hear of such things. Nobody in Colorado planted gardens, Father Vaillant related; nobody would stick a shovel into the earth for anything less than gold. There was no butter, no milk, no eggs, no fruit. He lived on dough and cured hog meat.

Within a few weeks after his arrival, six feather-beds were sent to the Bishop's house for Father Vaillant; dozens of linen sheets, embroidered pillow-cases and table-cloths and napkins; strings of chili and boxes of beans and dried fruit. The little settlement of Chimayo sent a roll of their finest blankets.

As these gifts arrived, Father Joseph put them in the woodhouse, knowing well that the Bishop was always embarrassed by his readiness to receive presents. But one morning Father Latour had occasion to go into the woodhouse, and he saw for himself.

"Father Joseph," he remonstrated, "you will never be able to take all these things back to Denver. Why, you would need an ox-cart to carry them!"

"Very well," replied Father Joseph, "then God will send me an ox-cart."

And He did, with a driver to take the cart as far as Pueblo.

On the morning of his departure for home, when his carriage was ready, the cart covered with tarpaulins and the oxen yoked, Father Vaillant, who had been hurrying everyone since the first streak of light, suddenly became deliberate. He went into the Bishop's study and sat down, talking to him of unimportant matters, lingering as if there were something still undone.

"Well, we are getting older, Jean," he said abruptly, after a short silence.

The Bishop smiled. "Ah, yes. We are not young men any more. One of these departures will be the last."

Father Vaillant nodded. "Whenever God wills. I am ready." He rose and began to pace the floor, addressing his friend without looking at him. "But it has not been so bad, Jean? We have done the things we used to plan to do, long ago, when we were Seminarians, — at least some of them. To fulfil the

263

dreams of one's youth; that is the best that can happen to a man. No worldly success can take the place of that."

"*Blanchet*," said the Bishop rising, "you are a better man than I. You have been a great harvester of souls, without pride and without shame — and I am always a little cold — *un pédant*, as you used to say. If hereafter we have stars in our crowns, yours will be a constellation. Give me your blessing."

He knelt, and Father Vaillant, having blessed him, knelt and was blessed in turn. They embraced each other for the past — for the future.

BOOK NINE

DEATH COMES FOR THE ARCHBISHOP

1

WHEN that devout nun, Mother Superior Philo-mène, died at a great age in her native Riom, among her papers were found several letters from Archbishop Latour, one dated December 1888, only a few months before his death. "*Since your brother was called to his reward,*" he wrote, "*I feel nearer to him than before. For many years Duty separated us, but death has brought us together. The time is not far distant when I shall join him. Meanwhile, I am enjoying to the full that period of reflection which is the happiest conclusion to a life of action.*"

This period of reflection the Archbishop spent on his little country estate, some four miles north of Santa Fé. Long before his retirement from the cares of the diocese, Father Latour bought those few acres in the red sand-hills near the Tesuque pueblo, and set out an orchard which would be bearing when the time came for him to rest. He chose this place in the red hills spotted with juniper against the advice of his friends, because he believed it to be admirably suited for the growing of fruit.

Once when he was riding out to visit the Tesuque mission, he had followed a stream and come upon this spot, where he found a little Mexican house and a garden shaded by an apricot tree of such great size as he had never seen before. It had two trunks, each of them thicker than a man's body, and though evidently very old, it was full of fruit. The apricots were large, beautifully coloured, and of superb flavour. Since this tree grew against the hillside, the Archbishop concluded that the exposure there must be excellent for fruit. He surmised that the heat of the sun, reflected from the rocky hill-slope up into the tree, gave the fruit an even temperature, warmth from two sides, such as brings the wall peaches to perfection in France.

The old Mexican who lived there said the tree must be two hundred years old; it had been just like this when his grandfather was a boy, and had always borne luscious apricots like these. The old man would be glad to sell the place and move into Santa Fé, the Bishop found, and he bought it a few weeks later. In the spring he set out his orchard and a few rows of acacia trees. Some years afterward he built a little adobe house, with a chapel, high up on the hill-side overlooking the orchard. Thither he used to go for rest and at seasons of special devotion. After his retirement, he went there to live, though he always kept his study unchanged in the house of the new Archbishop.

In his retirement Father Latour's principal work was the training of the new missionary priests who arrived from France. His successor, the second Archbishop, was also an Auvergnat, from Father Latour's own college, and the clergy of northern New Mexico remained predominantly French. When a company of new priests arrived (they never came singly) Archbishop S—— sent them out to stay with Father Latour for a few months, to receive instruction in Spanish, in the topography of the diocese, in the character and traditions of the different pueblos.

Father Latour's recreation was his garden. He grew such fruit as was hardly to be found even in the old orchards of California; cherries and apricots, apples and quinces, and the peerless pears of France — even the most delicate varieties. He urged the new priests to plant fruit trees wherever they went, and to encourage the Mexicans to add fruit to their starchy diet. Wherever there was a French priest, there should be a garden of fruit trees and vegetables and flowers. He often quoted to his students that passage from their fellow Auvergnat, Pascal: that Man was lost and saved in a garden.

He domesticated and developed the native wild flowers. He had one hill-side solidly clad with that low-growing purple verbena which mats over the hills of New Mexico. It was like a great violet velvet mantle thrown down in the sun; all the shades that the dyers and weavers of Italy and France strove for through centuries, the violet that is full of rose colour and is yet not lavender; the blue that becomes almost pink and then retreats again into sea-dark purple — the true Episcopal colour and countless variations of it.

In the year 1885 there came to New Mexico a young Seminarian, Bernard Ducrot, who became like a son to Father Latour. The story of the old Archbishop's life, often told in the cloisters and class-rooms at Montferrand, had taken hold of this boy's imagination, and he had long waited an opportunity to come. Bernard was handsome in person and of unusual mentality, had in himself the fineness to reverence all that was fine in his venerable Superior. He anticipated Father Latour's every wish, shared his reflections, cherished his reminiscences.

"Surely," the Bishop used to say to the priests, "God himself has sent me this young man to help me through the last years."

2

Throughout the autumn of the year '88 the Bishop was in good health. He had five French priests in his house, and he still rode abroad with them to visit the nearer missions. On Christmas eve, he performed the midnight Mass in the Cathedral at Santa Fé. In January he drove with Bernard to Santa Cruz to see the resident priest, who was ill. While they were on their way home the weather suddenly changed, and a violent rain-storm overtook them. They were in an open buggy and were drenched to the skin before they could reach any Mexican house for shelter.

After arriving home, Father Latour went at once to bed. During the night he slept badly and felt feverish. He called none of his household, but arose at the usual hour before dawn and went into the chapel for his devotions. While he was at prayer, he was seized with a chill. He made his way to the kitchen, and his old cook, Fructosa, alarmed at once, put him to bed and gave him brandy. This chill left him feverish, and he developed a distressing cough.

After keeping quietly to his bed for a few days, the Bishop called young Bernard to him one morning and said:

DEATH COMES FOR THE ARCHBISHOP

"Bernard, will you ride into Santa Fé to-day and see the Archbishop for me. Ask him whether it will be quite convenient if I return to occupy my study in his house for a short time. *Je voudrais mourir à Santa Fé.*"

"I will go at once, Father. But you should not be discouraged; one does not die of a cold."

The old man smiled. "I shall not die of a cold, my son. I shall die of having lived."

From that moment on, he spoke only French to those about him, and this sudden relaxing of his rule alarmed his household more than anything else about his condition. When a priest had received bad news from home, or was ill, Father Latour would converse with him in his own language; but at other times he required that all conversation in his house should be in Spanish or English.

Bernard returned that afternoon to say that the Archbishop would be delighted if Father Latour would remain the rest of the winter with him. Magdalena had already begun to air his study and put it in order, and she would be in special attendance upon him during his visit. The Archbishop would send his new carriage to fetch him, as Father Latour had only an open buggy.

"Not to-day, *mon fils*," said the Bishop. "We will choose a day when I am feeling stronger; a fair day, when we can go in my own buggy, and you can drive me. I wish to go late in the afternoon, toward sunset."

Bernard understood. He knew that once, long ago, at that hour of the day, a young Bishop had ridden along the Albuquerque road and seen Santa Fé for the first time. . . And often, when they were driving into town together, the Bishop had paused with Bernard on that hill-top from which Father Vaillant had looked back on Santa Fé, when he went away to Colorado to begin the work that had taken the rest of his life and made him, too, a Bishop in the end.

The old town was better to look at in those days, Father Latour used to tell Bernard with a sigh. In the old days it had an individuality, a style of its own; a tawny adobe town with a few green trees, set in a half-circle of carnelian-coloured hills; that and no more. But the year 1880 had begun a period of incongruous American building. Now, half the plaza square was still adobe, and half was flimsy wooden buildings with double porches, scroll-work and jack-straw posts and banisters painted white. Father Latour said the wooden houses which had so distressed him in Ohio, had followed him. All this was quite wrong for the Cathedral he had been so many years in building, — the Cathedral that had taken Father Vaillant's place in his life after that remarkable man went away.

DEATH COMES FOR THE ARCHBISHOP

Father Latour made his last entry into Santa Fé at the end of a brilliant February afternoon; Bernard stopped the horses at the foot of the long street to await the sunset.

Wrapped in his Indian blankets, the old Archbishop sat for a long while, looking at the open, golden face of his Cathedral. How exactly young Molny, his French architect, had done what he wanted! Nothing sensational, simply honest building and good stone-cutting, — good Midi Romanesque of the plainest. And even now, in winter, when the acacia trees before the door were bare, how it was of the South, that church, how it sounded the note of the South!

No one but Molny and the Bishop had ever seemed to enjoy the beautiful site of that building, — perhaps no one ever would. But these two had spent many an hour admiring it. The steep carnelian hills drew up so close behind the church that the individual pine trees thinly wooding their slopes were clearly visible. From the end of the street where the Bishop's buggy stood, the tawny church seemed to start directly out of those rose-coloured hills — with a purpose so strong that it was like action. Seen from this distance, the Cathedral lay against the pine-splashed slopes as against a curtain. When Bernard drove slowly nearer, the backbone of the hills sank gradually, and the towers rose clear into the blue air, while the body of the church still lay against the mountain.

The young architect used to tell the Bishop that only in Italy, or in the opera, did churches leap out of mountains and black pines like that. More than once Molny had called the Bishop from his study to look at the unfinished building when a storm was coming up; then the sky above the mountain grew black, and the carnelian rocks became an intense lavender, all their pine trees strokes of dark purple; the hills drew nearer, the whole background approached like a dark threat.

"Setting," Molny used to tell Father Latour, "is accident. Either a building is a part of a place, or it is not. Once that kinship is there, time will only make it stronger."

The Bishop was recalling this saying of Molny's when a voice out of the present sounded in his ear. It was Bernard.

"A fine sunset, Father. See how red the mountains are growing; Sangre de Cristo."

Yes, Sangre de Cristo; but no matter how scarlet the sunset, those red hills never became vermilion, but a more and more intense rose-carnelian; not the colour of living blood, the Bishop had often reflected, but the colour of the dried blood of saints and martyrs preserved in old churches in Rome, which liquefies upon occasion.

DEATH COMES FOR THE ARCHBISHOP

3

THE next morning Father Latour wakened with a grateful sense of nearness to his Cathedral — which would also be his tomb. He felt safe under its shadow; like a boat come back to harbour, lying under its own sea-wall. He was in his old study; the Sisters had sent a little iron bed from the school for him, and their finest linen and blankets. He felt a great content at being here, where he had come as a young man and where he had done his work. The room was little changed; the same rugs and skins on the earth floor, the same desk with his candlesticks, the same thick, wavy white walls that muted sound, that shut out the world and gave repose to the spirit.

As the darkness faded into the grey of a winter morning, he listened for the church bells, — and for another sound, that always amused him here; the whistle of a locomotive. Yes, he had come with the buffalo, and he had lived to see railway trains running into Santa Fé. He had accomplished an historic period.

All his relatives at home, and his friends in New Mexico, had expected that the old Archbishop would spend his closing years in France, probably in Clermont, where he could occupy a chair in his old

274

college. That seemed the natural thing to do, and he had given it grave consideration. He had half expected to make some such arrangement the last time he was in Auvergne, just before his retirement from his duties as Archbishop. But in the Old World he found himself homesick for the New. It was a feeling he could not explain; a feeling that old age did not weigh so heavily upon a man in New Mexico as in the Puy-de-Dôm.

He loved the towering peaks of his native mountains, the comeliness of the villages, the cleanness of the country-side, the beautiful lines and the cloisters of his own college. Clermont was beautiful, — but he found himself sad there; his heart lay like a stone in his breast. There was too much past, perhaps ... When the summer wind stirred the lilacs in the old gardens and shook down the blooms of the horse-chestnuts, he sometimes closed his eyes and thought of the high song the wind was singing in the straight, striped pine trees up in the Navajo forests.

During the day his nostalgia wore off, and by dinner-time it was quite gone. He enjoyed his dinner and his wine, and the company of cultivated men, and usually retired in good spirits. It was in the early morning that he felt the ache in his breast; it had something to do with waking in the early morning. It seemed to him that the grey dawn lasted so long here, the country was a long while in coming to life. The gardens and the fields were damp, heavy mists hung in the valley and obscured the mountains; hours went by before the sun could disperse those vapours and warm and purify the villages.

In New Mexico he always awoke a young man; not until he rose and began to shave did he realize that he was growing older. His first consciousness was a sense of the light dry wind blowing in through the windows, with the fragrance of hot sun and sage-brush and sweet clover; a wind that made one's body feel light and one's heart cry "To-day, to-day," like a child's.

Beautiful surroundings, the society of learned men, the charm of noble women, the graces of art, could not make up to him for the loss of those light-hearted mornings of the desert, for that wind that made one a boy again. He had noticed that this peculiar quality in the air of new countries vanished after they were tamed by man and made to bear harvests. Parts of Texas and Kansas that he had first known as open range had since been made into rich farming districts, and the air had quite lost that lightness, that dry aromatic odour. The moisture of plowed land, the heaviness of labour and growth and grain-bearing, utterly destroyed it; one could breathe that only on the bright edges of the world, on the great grass plains or the sage-brush desert.

That air would disappear from the whole earth

in time, perhaps; but long after his day. He did not know just when it had become so necessary to him, but he had come back to die in exile for the sake of it. Something soft and wild and free, something that whispered to the ear on the pillow, lightened the heart, softly, softly picked the lock, slid the bolts, and released the prisoned spirit of man into the wind, into the blue and gold, into the morning, into the morning!

4

FATHER LATOUR arranged an order for his last days; if routine was necessary to him in health, it was even more so in sickness. Early in the morning Bernard came with hot water, shaved him, and helped him to bathe. They had brought nothing in from the country with them but clothing and linen, and the silver toilet articles the Olivares had given the Bishop so long ago; these thirty years he had washed his hands in that hammered basin. Morning prayers over, Magdalena came with his breakfast, and he sat in his easy-chair while she made his bed and arranged his room. Then he was ready to see visitors.

277

DEATH COMES FOR THE ARCHBISHOP

The Archbishop came in for a few moments, when he was at home; the Mother Superior, the American doctor. Bernard read aloud to him the rest of the morning; St. Augustine, or the letters of Madame de Sevigné, or his favourite Pascal.

Sometimes, in the morning hours, he dictated to his young disciple certain facts about the old missions in the diocese; facts which he had come upon by chance and feared would be forgotten. He wished he could do this systematically, but he had not the strength. Those truths and fancies relating to a bygone time would probably be lost; the old legends and customs and superstitions were already dying out. He wished now that long ago he had had the leisure to write them down, that he could have arrested their flight by throwing about them the light and elastic mesh of the French tongue.

He had, indeed, for years, directed the thoughts of the young priests whom he instructed to the fortitude and devotion of those first missionaries, the Spanish friars; declaring that his own life, when he first came to New Mexico, was one of ease and comfort compared with theirs. If he had used to be abroad for weeks together on short rations, sleeping in the open, unable to keep his body clean, at least he had the sense of being in a friendly world, where by every man's fireside a welcome awaited him.

But the Spanish Fathers who came up to Zuñi,

then went north to the Navajos, west to the Hopis, east to all the pueblos scattered between Albuquerque and Taos, they came into a hostile country, carrying little provisionment but their breviary and crucifix. When their mules were stolen by Indians, as often happened, they proceeded on foot, without a change of raiment, without food or water. A European could scarcely imagine such hardships. The old countries were worn to the shape of human life, made into an investiture, a sort of second body, for man. There the wild herbs and the wild fruits and the forest fungi were edible. The streams were sweet water, the trees afforded shade and shelter. But in the alkali deserts the water holes were poisonous, and the vegetation offered nothing to a starving man. Everything was dry, prickly, sharp; Spanish bayonet, juniper, greasewood, cactus; the lizard, the rattle-snake, — and man made cruel by a cruel life. Those early missionaries threw themselves naked upon the hard heart of a country that was calculated to try the endurance of giants. They thirsted in its deserts, starved among its rocks, climbed up and down its terrible canyons on stone-bruised feet, broke long fasts by unclean and repugnant food. Surely these endured *Hunger, Thirst, Cold, Nakedness*, of a kind beyond any conception St. Paul and his brethren could have had. Whatever the early Christians suffered, it all happened in that safe little Mediterranean world, amid the old manners, the old landmarks. If they endured martyrdom, they died among their brethren, their relics were piously preserved, their names lived in the mouths of holy men.

Riding with his Auvergnats to the old missions that had been scenes of martyrdom, the Bishop used to remind them that no man could know what triumphs of faith had happened there, where one white man met torture and death alone among so many infidels, or what visions and revelations God may have granted to soften that brutal end.

When, as a young man, Father Latour first went down into Old Mexico, to claim his See at the hands of the Bishop of Durango, he had met on his journey priests from the missions of Sonora and Lower California, who related many stories of the blessed experiences of the early Franciscan missionaries. Their way through the wilderness had blossomed with little miracles, it seemed. At one time, when the renowned Father Junípero Serra, and his two companions, were in danger of their lives from trying to cross a river at a treacherous point, a mysterious stranger appeared out of the rocks on the opposite shore, and calling to them in Spanish, told them to follow him to a point farther up the stream, where they forded in safety. When they begged to know his name, he evaded them and disappeared. At another time, they were traversing a great plain, and were famished for water and almost spent; a young horseman overtook them and gave them three ripe pomegranates, then galloped away. This fruit not only quenched their thirst, but revived and strengthened them as much as the most nourishing food could have done, and they completed their journey like fresh men.

One night in his travels through Durango, Father Latour was entertained at a great country estate where the resident chaplain happened to be a priest from one of the western missions; and he told a story of this same Father Junípero which had come down in his own monastery from the old times.

Father Junípero, he said, with a single companion, had once arrived at his monastery on foot, without provisions. The Brothers had welcomed the two in astonishment, believing it impossible that men could have crossed so great a stretch of desert in this naked fashion. The Superior questioned them as to whence they had come, and said the mission should not have allowed them to set off without a guide and without food. He marvelled how they could have got through alive. But Father Junípero replied that they had fared very well, and had been most agreeably entertained by a poor Mexican family on the way. At this a muleteer, who was bringing in wood for the Brothers, began to laugh, and said there was no house for twelve leagues, nor anyone at all living in the sandy waste through which they had come; and the Brothers confirmed him in this.

Then Father Junípero and his companion related fully their adventure. They had set out with bread and water for one day. But on the second day they had been travelling since dawn across a cactus desert and had begun to lose heart when, near sunset, they espied in the distance three great cottonwood trees, very tall in the declining light. Toward these they hastened. As they approached the trees, which were large and green and were shedding cotton freely, they observed an ass tied to a dead trunk which stuck up out of the sand. Looking about for the owner of the ass, they came upon a little Mexican house with an oven by the door and strings of red peppers hanging on the wall. When they called aloud, a venerable Mexican, clad in sheepskins, came out and greeted them kindly, asking them to stay the night. Going in with him, they observed that all was neat and comely, and the wife, a young woman of beautiful countenance, was stirring porridge by the fire. Her child, scarcely more than an infant and with no garment but his little shirt, was on the floor beside her, playing with a pet lamb.

They found these people gentle, pious, and well-spoken. The husband said they were shepherds. The priests sat at their table and shared their supper, and afterward read the evening prayers. They had wished to question the host about the country, and about his mode of life and where he found pasture for his flock, but they were overcome by a great and sweet weariness, and taking each a sheepskin provided him, they lay down upon the floor and sank into deep sleep. When they awoke in the morning they found all as before, and food set upon the table, but the family were absent, even to the pet lamb, — having gone, the Fathers supposed, to care for their flock.

When the Brothers at the monastery heard this account they were amazed, declaring that there were indeed three cottonwood trees growing together in the desert, a well-known landmark; but that if a settler had come, he must have come very lately. So Father Junípero and Father Andrea, his companion, with some of the Brothers and the scoffing muleteer, went back into the wilderness to prove the matter. The three tall trees they found, shedding their cotton, and the dead trunk to which the ass had been tied. But the ass was not there, nor any house, nor the oven by the door. Then the two Fathers sank down upon their knees in that blessed spot and kissed the earth, for they perceived what Family it was that had entertained them there.

Father Junípero confessed to the Brothers how from the moment he entered the house he had been strangely drawn to the child, and desired to take him in his arms, but that he kept near his mother. When the priest was reading the evening prayers the child sat upon the floor against his mother's knee, with the lamb in his lap, and the Father found it hard to keep his eyes upon his breviary. After prayers, when he bade his hosts good-night, he did indeed stoop over the little boy in blessing; and the child had lifted his hand, and with his tiny finger made the cross upon Father Junípero's forehead.

This story of Father Junípero's Holy Family made a strong impression upon the Bishop, when it was told him by the fireside of that great hacienda where he was a guest for the night. He had such an affection for that story, indeed, that he had allowed himself to repeat it on but two occasions; once to the nuns of Mother Philomène's convent in Riom, and once at a dinner given by Cardinal Mazzucchi, in Rome. There is always something charming in the idea of greatness returning to simplicity — the queen making hay among the country girls — but how much more endearing was the belief that They, after so many centuries of history and glory, should return to play Their first parts, in the persons of a humble Mexican family, the lowliest of the lowly, the poorest of the poor, — in a wilderness at the end of the world, where the angels could scarcely find Them!

DEATH COMES FOR THE ARCHBISHOP

5

Aᴛᴛᴇʀ his *déjeuner* the old Archbishop made a
pretence of sleeping. He requested not to be dis-
turbed until dinner-time, and those long hours of
solitude were precious to him. His bed was at the
dark end of the room, where the shadows were rest-
ful to his eyes; on fair days the other end was full of
sunlight, on grey days the light of the fire flickered
along the wavy white walls. Lying so still that the
bed-clothes over his body scarcely moved, with his
hands resting delicately on the sheet beside him or
upon his breast, the Bishop was living over his life.
When he was otherwise motionless, the thumb of his
right hand would sometimes gently touch a ring on
his forefinger, an amethyst with an inscription cut
upon it, *Auspice Maria,* — Father Vaillant's signet-
ring; and then he was almost certainly thinking of
Joseph; of their life together here, in this room . . .
in Ohio beside the Great Lakes . . . as young men in
Paris . . . as boys at Montferrand. There were many
passages in their missionary life that he loved to
recall; and how often and how fondly he recalled the
beginning of it!

They were both young men in their twenties,
curates to older priests, when there came to Clermont

a Bishop from Ohio, a native of Auvergne, looking
for volunteers for his missions in the West. Father
Jean and Father Joseph heard him lecture at the
Seminary, and talked with him in private. Before
he left for the North, they had pledged themselves
to meet him in Paris at a given date, to spend some
weeks of preparation at the College for Foreign
Missions in the rue du Bac, and then to sail with him
from Cherbourg.

Both the young priests knew that their families
would strongly oppose their purpose, so they resolved
to reveal it to no one; to make no adieux, but to steal
away disguised in civilian's clothes. They comforted
each other by recalling that St. Francis Xavier,
when he set forth as missionary to India, had stolen
away like this; had *"passed the dwelling of his
parents without saluting them,"* as they had learned
at school; terrible words to a French boy.

Father Vaillant's position was especially painful;
his father was a stern, silent man, long a widower,
who loved his children with a jealous passion and
had no life but in their lives. Joseph was the eldest
child. The period between his resolve and its execution was a period of anguish for him. As the date
set for their departure drew near, he grew thinner
and paler than ever.

By agreement the two friends were to meet at
dawn in a certain field outside Riom on the fateful

day, and there await the *diligence* for Paris. Jean Latour, having made his decision and pledged himself, knew no wavering. On the appointed morning he stole out of his sister's house and took his way through the sleeping town to that mountain field, tip-tilted by reason of its steepness, just beginning to show a cold green in the heavy light of a cloudy day-break. There he found his comrade in a miserable plight. Joseph had been abroad in the fields all night, wandering up and down, finding his purpose and losing it. His face was swollen with weeping. He shook with a chill, his voice was beyond his control.

"What shall I do, Jean? Help me!" he cried. "I cannot break my father's heart, and I cannot break the vow I have made to Heaven. I had rather die than do either. Ah, if I could but die of this misery, here, now!"

How clearly the old Archbishop could recall the scene; those two young men in the fields in the grey morning, disguised as if they were criminals, escaping by stealth from their homes. He had not known how to comfort his friend; it seemed to him that Joseph was suffering more than flesh could bear, that he was actually being torn in two by conflicting desires. While they were pacing up and down, arm-in-arm, they heard a hollow sound; the *diligence* rumbling down the mountain gorge. Joseph stood still and buried his face in his hands. The postilion's horn sounded.

"*Allons!*" said Jean lightly. "*L'invitation du voyage!* You will accompany me to Paris. Once we are there, if your father is not reconciled, we will get Bishop F—— to absolve you from your promise, and you can return to Riom. It is very simple."

He ran to the road-side and waved to the driver; the coach stopped. In a moment they were off, and before long Joseph had fallen asleep in his seat from sheer exhaustion. But he always said that if Jean Latour had not supported him in that hour of torment, he would have been a parish priest in the Puy de Dom for the rest of his life.

Of the two young priests who set forth from Riom that morning in early spring, Jean Latour had seemed the one so much more likely to succeed in a missionary's life. He, indeed, had a sound mind in a sound body. During the weeks they spent at the College of Foreign Missions in the rue du Bac, the authorities had been very doubtful of Joseph's fitness for the hardships of the mission field. Yet in the long test of years it was that frail body that had endured more and accomplished more.

Father Latour often said that his diocese changed little except in boundaries. The Mexicans were always Mexicans, the Indians were always Indians. Santa Fé was a quiet backwater, with no natural wealth, no importance commercially. But Father Vaillant had been plunged into the midst of a great industrial expansion, where guile and trickery and honourable ambition all struggled together; a territory that developed by leaps and bounds and then experienced ruinous reverses. Every year, even after he was crippled, he travelled thousands of miles by stage and in his carriage, among the mountain towns that were now rich, now poor and deserted; Boulder, Gold Hill, Caribou, Cache-à-la-Poudre, Spanish Bar, South Park, up the Arkansas to Cache Creek and California Gulch.

And Father Vaillant had not been content to be a mere missionary priest. He became a promoter. He saw a great future for the Church in Colorado. While he was still so poor that he could not have a rectory of ordinary comfort to live in, he began buying up great tracts of land for the Church. He was able to buy a great deal of land for very little money, but that little had to be borrowed from banks at a ruinous rate of interest. He borrowed money to build schools and convents, and the interest on his debts ate him up. He made long begging trips through Ohio and Pennsylvania and Canada to raise money to pay this interest, which grew like a rolling snowball. He formed a land company, went abroad and floated bonds in France to raise money, and dishonest brokers brought reproach upon his name.

DEATH COMES FOR THE ARCHBISHOP

When he was nearly seventy, with one leg four inches shorter than the other, Father Vaillant, then first Bishop of Colorado, was summoned to Rome to explain his complicated finance before the Papal court, — and he had very hard work to satisfy the Cardinals.

When a dispatch was flashed into Santa Fé announcing Bishop Vaillant's death, Father Latour at once took the new railroad for Denver. But he could scarcely believe the telegram. He recalled the old nickname, Trompe-la-Mort, and remembered how many times before he had hurried across mountains and deserts, not daring to hope he would find his friend alive.

Curiously, Father Latour could never feel that he had actually been present at Father Joseph's funeral — or rather, he could not believe that Father Joseph was there. The shrivelled little old man in the coffin, scarcely larger than a monkey — that had nothing to do with Father Vaillant. He could see Joseph as clearly as he could see Bernard, but always as he was when they first came to New Mexico. It was not sentiment; that was the picture of Father Joseph his memory produced for him, and it did not produce any other. The funeral itself, he liked to remember — as a recognition. It was held under canvas, in the open air; there was not a building in Denver —

in the whole Far West, for that matter, — big enough for his *Blanchet's* funeral. For two days before, the populations of villages and mining camps had been streaming down the mountains; they slept in wagons and tents and barns; they made a throng like a National Convention in the convent square. And a strange thing happened at that funeral:

Father Revardy, the French priest who had gone from Santa Fé to Colorado with Father Vaillant more than twenty years before, and had been with him ever since as his curate and Vicar, had been sent to France on business for his Bishop. While there, he was told by his physician that he had a fatal malady, and he at once took ship and hurried homeward, to make his report to Bishop Vaillant and to die in the harness. When he got as far as Chicago, he had an acute seizure and was taken to a Catholic hospital, where he lay very ill. One morning a nurse happened to leave a newspaper near his bed; glancing at it, Father Revardy saw an announcement of the death of the Bishop of Colorado. When the Sister returned, she found her patient dressed. He convinced her that he must be driven to the railway station at once. On reaching Denver he entered a carriage and asked to be taken to the Bishop's funeral. He arrived there when the services were nearly half over, and no one ever forgot the sight of this dying man, supported by the cab-driver and two priests, making his way through the crowd and dropping upon his knees beside the bier. A chair was brought for him, and for the rest of the ceremony he sat with his forehead resting against the edge of the coffin. When Bishop Vaillant was carried away to his tomb, Father Revardy was taken to the hospital, where he died a few days later. It was one more instance of the extraordinary personal devotion that Father Joseph had so often aroused and retained so long, in red men and yellow men and white.

6

DURING those last weeks of the Bishop's life he thought very little about death; it was the Past he was leaving. The future would take care of itself. But he had an intellectual curiosity about dying; about the changes that took place in a man's beliefs and scale of values. More and more life seemed to him an experience of the Ego, in no sense the Ego itself. This conviction, he believed, was something apart from his religious life; it was an enlightenment that came to him as a man, a human creature. And he noticed that he judged conduct differently now; his own and that of others. The mistakes of his life seemed unimportant; accidents that had occurred *en route*, like the shipwreck in Galveston harbour, or the runaway in which he was hurt when he was first on his way to New Mexico in search of his Bishopric.

He observed also that there was no longer any perspective in his memories. He remembered his winters with his cousins on the Mediterranean when he was a little boy, his student days in the Holy City, as clearly as he remembered the arrival of M. Molny and the building of his Cathedral. He was soon to have done with calendared time, and it had already ceased to count for him. He sat in the middle of his own consciousness; none of his former states of mind were lost or outgrown. They were all within reach of his hand, and all comprehensible.

Sometimes, when Magdalena or Bernard came in and asked him a question, it took him several seconds to bring himself back to the present. He could see they thought his mind was failing; but it was only extraordinarily active in some other part of the great picture of his life — some part of which they knew nothing.

When the occasion warranted he could return to the present. But there was not much present left; Father Joseph dead, the Olivares both dead, Kit Carson dead, only the minor characters of his life remained in present time. One morning, several weeks after the Bishop came back to Santa Fé, one of the strong people of the old deep days of life did appear, not in memory but in the flesh, in the shallow light of the present; Eusabio the Navajo. Out on the Colorado Chiquito he had heard the word, passed on from one trading post to another, that the old Archbishop was failing, and the Indian came to Santa Fé. He, too, was an old man now. Once again their fine hands clasped. The Bishop brushed a drop of moisture from his eye.

"I have wished for this meeting, my friend. I had thought of asking you to come, but it is a long way."

The old Navajo smiled. "Not long now, any more. I come on the cars, Padre. I get on the cars at Gallup, and the same day I am here. You remember when we come together once to Santa Fé from my country? How long it take us? Two weeks, pretty near. Men travel faster now, but I do not know if they go to better things."

"We must not try to know the future, Eusabio. It is better not. And Manuelito?"

"Manuelito is well; he still leads his people."

Eusabio did not stay long, but he said he would come again to-morrow, as he had business in Santa Fé that would keep him for some days. He had no business there; but when he looked at Father Latour he said to himself, "It will not be long."

After he was gone, the Bishop turned to Bernard; "My son, I have lived to see two great wrongs righted; I have seen the end of black slavery, and I have seen the Navajos restored to their own country."

For many years Father Latour used to wonder if there would ever be an end to the Indian wars while there was one Navajo or Apache left alive. Too many traders and manufacturers made a rich profit out of that warfare; a political machine and immense capital were employed to keep it going.

———

7

The Bishop's middle years in New Mexico had been clouded by the persecution of the Navajos and their expulsion from their own country. Through his friendship with Eusabio he had become interested in the Navajos soon after he first came to his new diocese, and he admired them; they stirred his imagination. Though this nomad people were much slower to adopt white man's ways than the home-staying Indians who dwelt in pueblos, and were much more indifferent to missionaries and the white man's religion, Father Latour felt a superior strength in them. There was purpose and conviction behind their inscrutable reserve; something active and quick, something with an edge. The expulsion of the Navajos from their country, which had been theirs no man knew how long, had seemed to him an injustice that cried to Heaven. Never could he forget that terrible winter when they were being hunted down and driven by thousands from their own reservation to the Bosque Redondo, three hundred miles away on the Pecos River. Hundreds of them, men, women, and children, perished from hunger and cold on the way; their sheep and horses died from exhaustion crossing the mountains. None ever went willingly; they were driven by starvation and the bayonet; captured in isolated bands, and brutally deported.

It was his own misguided friend, Kit Carson, who finally subdued the last unconquered remnant of that people; who followed them into the depths of the Canyon de Chelly, whither they had fled from their grazing plains and pine forests to make their last stand. They were shepherds, with no property but their live-stock, encumbered by their women and children, poorly armed and with scanty ammunition. But this canyon had always before proved impenetrable to white troops. The Navajos believed it could not be taken. They believed that their old gods dwelt in the fastnesses of that canyon; like

their Shiprock, it was an inviolate place, the very heart and centre of their life.

Carson followed them down into the hidden world between those towering walls of red sandstone, spoiled their stores, destroyed their deep-sheltered corn-fields, cut down the terraced peach orchards so dear to them. When they saw all that was sacred to them laid waste, the Navajos lost heart. They did not surrender; they simply ceased to fight, and were taken. Carson was a soldier under orders, and he did a soldier's brutal work. But the bravest of the Navajo chiefs he did not capture. Even after the crushing defeat of his people in the Canyon de Chelly, Manuelito was still at large. It was then that Eusabio came to Santa Fé to ask Bishop Latour to meet Manuelito at Zuñi. As a priest, the Bishop knew that it was indiscreet to consent to a meeting with this outlawed chief; but he was a man, too, and a lover of justice. The request came to him in such a way that he could not refuse it. He went with Eusabio.

Though the Government was offering a heavy reward for his person, living or dead, Manuelito rode off his own reservation down into Zuñi in broad daylight, attended by some dozen followers, all on wretched, half-starved horses. He had been in hiding out in Eusabio's country on the Colorado Chiquito.

It was Manuelito's hope that the Bishop would

go to Washington and plead his people's cause before they were utterly destroyed. They asked nothing of the Government, he told Father Latour, but their religion, and their own land where they had lived from immemorial times. Their country, he explained, was a part of their religion; the two were inseparable. The Canyon de Chelly the Padre knew; in that canyon his people had lived when they were a small weak tribe; it had nourished and protected them; it was their mother. Moreover, their gods dwelt there — in those inaccessible white houses set in caverns up in the face of the cliffs, which were older than the white man's world, and which no living man had ever entered. Their gods were there, just as the Padre's God was in his church.

And north of the Canyon de Chelly was the Shiprock, a slender crag rising to a dizzy height, all alone out on a flat desert. Seen at a distance of fifty miles or so, that crag presents the figure of a one-masted fishing-boat under full sail, and the white man named it accordingly. But the Indian has another name; he believes that rock was once a ship of the air. Ages ago, Manuelito told the Bishop, that crag had moved through the air, bearing upon its summit the parents of the Navajo race from the place in the far north where all peoples were made, — and wherever it sank to earth was to be their land. It sank in a desert country, where it

was hard for men to live. But they had found the Canyon de Chelly, where there was shelter and unfailing water. That canyon and the Shiprock were like kind parents to his people, places more sacred to them than churches, more sacred than any place is to the white man. How, then, could they go three hundred miles away and live in a strange land?

Moreover, the Bosque Redondo was down on the Pecos, far east of the Rio Grande. Manuelito drew a map in the sand, and explained to the Bishop how, from the very beginning, it had been enjoined that his people must never cross the Rio Grande on the east, or the Rio San Juan on the north, or the Rio Colorado on the west; if they did, the tribe would perish. If a great priest, like Father Latour, were to go to Washington and explain these things, perhaps the Government would listen.

Father Latour tried to tell the Indian that in a Protestant country the one thing a Roman priest could not do was to interfere in matters of Government. Manuelito listened respectfully, but the Bishop saw that he did not believe him. When he had finished, the Navajo rose and said:

"You are the friend of Cristobal, who hunts my people and drives them over the mountains to the Bosque Redondo. Tell your friend that he will never take me alive. He can come and kill me when he pleases. Two years ago I could not count my flocks;

now I have thirty sheep and a few starving horses. My children are eating roots, and I do not care for my life. But my mother and my gods are in the West, and I will never cross the Rio Grande."

He never did cross it. He lived in hiding until the return of his exiled people. For an unforeseen thing happened:

The Bosque Redondo proved an utterly unsuitable country for the Navajos. It could have been farmed by irrigation, but they were nomad shepherds, not farmers. There was no pasture for their flocks. There was no firewood; they dug mesquite roots and dried them for fuel. It was an alkaline country, and hundreds of Indians died from bad water. At last the Government at Washington admitted its mistake — which governments seldom do. After five years of exile, the remnant of the Navajo people were permitted to go back to their sacred places.

In 1875 the Bishop took his French architect on a pack trip into Arizona to show him something of the country before he returned to France, and he had the pleasure of seeing the Navajo horsemen riding free over their great plains again. The two Frenchmen went as far as the Canyon de Chelly to behold the strange cliff ruins; once more crops were growing down at the bottom of the world between the towering sandstone walls; sheep were grazing under the magnificent cottonwoods and drinking at the streams of sweet water; it was like an Indian Garden of Eden.

Now, when he was an old man and ill, scenes from those bygone times, dark and bright, flashed back to the Bishop: the terrible faces of the Navajos waiting at the place on the Rio Grande where they were being ferried across into exile; the long streams of survivors going back to their own country, driving their scanty flocks, carrying their old men and their children. Memories, too, of that time he had spent with Eusabio on the Little Colorado, in the early spring, when the lambing season was not yet over, — dark horsemen riding across the sands with orphan lambs in their arms — a young Navajo woman, giving a lamb her breast until a ewe was found for it.

"Bernard," the old Bishop would murmur, "God has been very good to let me live to see a happy issue to those old wrongs. I do not believe, as I once did, that the Indian will perish. I believe that God will preserve him."

8

THE American doctor was consulting with Archbishop S—— and the Mother Superior. "It is his heart that is the trouble now. I have been giving him small doses to stimulate it, but they no longer have any effect. I scarcely dare increase them; it might be fatal at once. But that is why you see such a change in him."

The change was that the old man did not want food, and that he slept, or seemed to sleep, nearly all the time. On the last day of his life his condition was pretty generally known. The Cathedral was full of people all day long, praying for him; nuns and old women, young men and girls, coming and going. The sick man had received the Viaticum early in the morning. Some of the Tesuque Indians, who had been his country neighbours, came into Santa Fé and sat all day in the Archbishop's courtyard listening for news of him; with them was Eusabio the Navajo. Fructosa and Tranquilino, his old servants, were with the supplicants in the Cathedral.

The Mother Superior and Magdalena and Bernard attended the sick man. There was little to do but to watch and pray, so peaceful and painless was his repose. Sometimes it was sleep, they knew from his re-

laxed features; then his face would assume personality, consciousness, even though his eyes did not open.

Toward the close of day, in the short twilight
after the candles were lighted, the old Bishop seemed
to become restless, moved a little, and began to
murmur; it was in the French tongue, but Bernard,
though he caught some words, could make nothing
of them. He knelt beside the bed: "What is it,
Father? I am here."

He continued to murmur, to move his hands a
little, and Magdalena thought he was trying to ask
for something, or to tell them something. But in
reality the Bishop was not there at all; he was standing in a tip-tilted green field among his native mountains, and he was trying to give consolation to a young
man who was being torn in two before his eyes by the
desire to go and the necessity to stay. He was trying to
forge a new Will in that devout and exhausted priest;
and the time was short, for the *diligence* for Paris
was already rumbling down the mountain gorge.

When the Cathedral bell tolled just after dark, the
Mexican population of Santa Fé fell upon their knees,
and all American Catholics as well. Many others who
did not kneel prayed in their hearts. Eusabio and the
Tesuque boys went quietly away to tell their people;
and the next morning the old Archbishop lay before
the high altar in the church he had built.

A NOTE ON THE TYPE IN WHICH THIS BOOK IS SET

This book is composed on the monotype in Old Style No. 31. This face is largely based on a series originally cut by the Bruce Foundry in the early seventies and that in its turn appears to have followed, in all essentials, the details of a face designed and cut, some years before, by the celebrated Edinburgh type founders, Miller and Richard. It has always been a popular and satisfactory face for book work because while it is compactly designed, so that a large number of words appear on a page, its compactness is not accompanied by any loss in legibility. Old Style No. 31, composed in a page gives a subdued color and even texture which makes it easily and comfortably read.

SET UP, ELECTROTYPED, PRINTED AND BOUND BY THE PLIMPTON PRESS, NORWOOD, MASS. · PAPER FURNISHED BY W. F. ETHERINGTON & CO., NEW YORK